Ten Traditional Jewish Children's Stories

Retold by Gloria Goldreich

Illustrated by Jeffrey Allon

PITSPOPANY

NEW YORK ◇ JERUSALEM

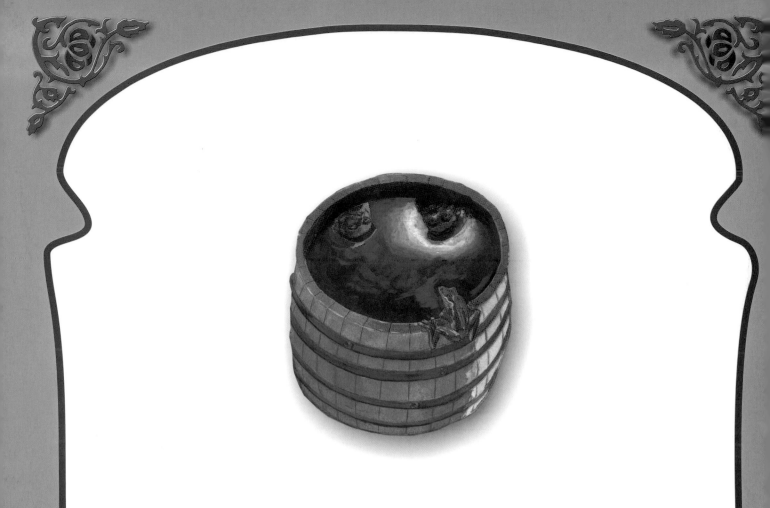

Published by PITSPOPANY PRESS
First cloth revised edition © 2000
Text Copyright © 1996 by Gloria Goldreich
Illustrations Copyright © 1996 by Jeffrey Allon

PRINTING HISTORY
First Impression, June 1996
Second Impression, June 2000

Pitspopany Press books may be purchased for educational
or special sales by contacting: Marketing Director,
Pitspopany Press, 40 East 78th Street, Suite 16D, New York, N. Y. 10021.
Fax: (212) 472-6253. E-mail: pop@netvision.net.il
Visit our website at: www.pitspopany.com

Design: Benjie Herskowitz

ISBN: 0-943706-69-6 Cloth
ISBN: 0-943706-87-4 Softcover

Printed in Hong Kong

For Hallel and Shelly

J.A.

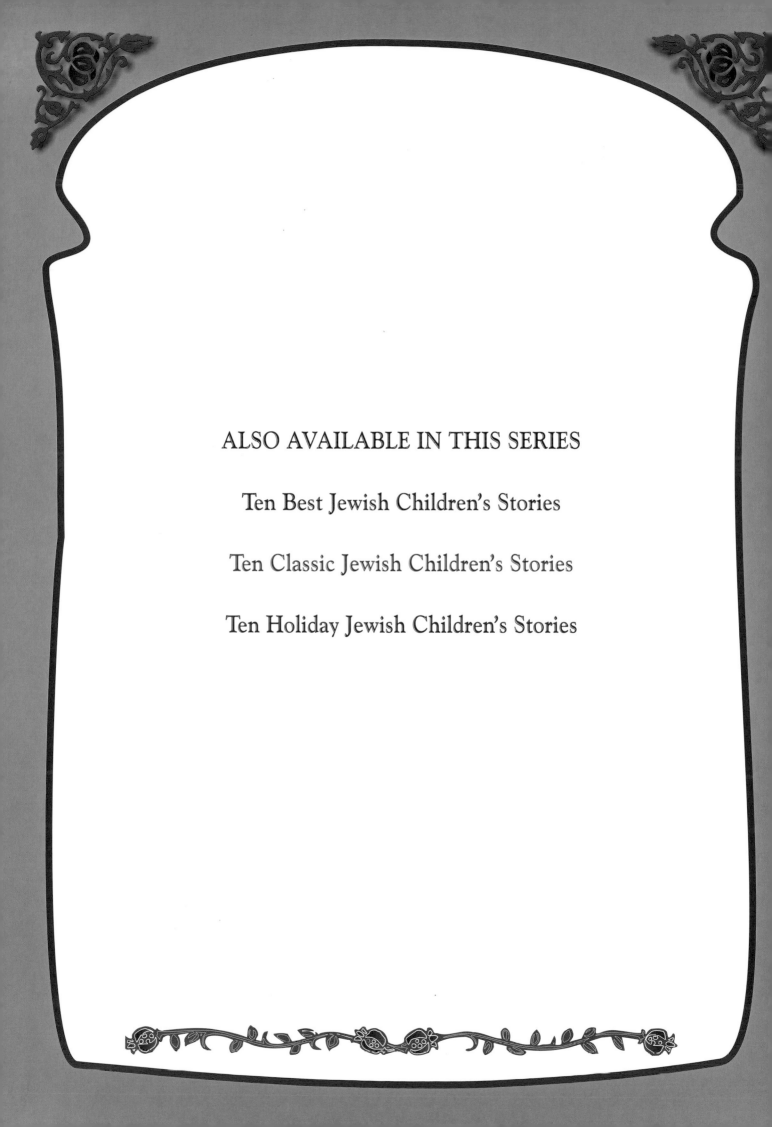

ALSO AVAILABLE IN THIS SERIES

Ten Best Jewish Children's Stories

Ten Classic Jewish Children's Stories

Ten Holiday Jewish Children's Stories

Table of Contents

Jewish Storytelling
by Howard Schwartz

*T*HE JEWISH PEOPLE ARE KNOWN AS THE PEOPLE OF THE BOOK but they might also be known as the People of the Stories. Jews have been a wandering people, but wherever they have gone, they have brought two things with them: their faith in the Torah that God gave them and their stories. Parents and grandparents told these stories to the children at night as they warmed themselves around the fire, and when they grew up, the children told these stories to their children. In this way the stories were passed down from one generation to the next.

Eventually many of these stories were written down and once the printing press was invented in the Middle Ages, books of these stories were published. Most of these books were written in Hebrew, but some of them were written in Yiddish because that was the language spoken by the Jews of Eastern Europe. One of the best known books was The *Ma'aseh* Book, which was published in Yiddish in the 16th century. A ma'aseh is a tale, and the people called these stories *buba-ma'asehs*, or "Grandmothers' Tales," because so many of the tales were told by grandmothers.

Now, there have been many great storytellers among the Jews, but perhaps the greatest of all was Rabbi Nachman of Bratslav, who lived in the 19th century. Rabbi Nachman was the great-grandson of the Ba'al Shem Tov, the founder of *Hasidism.*

The Ba'al Shem Tov was greatly beloved among the Jews, and many stories were told about him. One of these stories, "The Boy's Song," is included in this collection by Gloria Goldreich. The Ba'al Shem Tov believed that the most important thing in God's eyes was a person's true feelings. A person didn't have to be wealthy or educated in order to matter to God, since God looks into the heart. And we see this very clearly in the story of "The Boy's Song," where all the prayers of the adults fail to reach Heaven, but the boy's joyful playing on his flute sets their prayers free to ascend on high.

Perhaps because he was raised hearing so many stories about his great-grandfather, Rabbi Nachman became a storyteller himself. But the stories he told were not like the stories about the heroes of the Bible or the sages of old. They were very much like the buba-ma'asehs told among the people. They were much like fairy tales, but at the same time they contained much wisdom, and had a great deal to teach Rabbi Nachman's followers, known as his Hasidim.

Rabbi Nachman's stories became so famous and beloved among the people that they inspired modern Jewish writers to pay more attention to the folktales told among the people, and to try to retell them. The greatest of these writers was I. L. Peretz.

Peretz was close friends with S. Ansky, who was the first great Jewish folklorist. Ansky went on expeditions around Eastern Europe, where he collected many stories. When he returned from his travels, he would go to the house of his friend, Peretz, and tell him many of these stories. Then Peretz would sit at his desk and retell these newly collected tales.

There are two stories by Peretz in this collection. One is the story of "The Golem." Of all Jewish legends, this is perhaps the most famous. It tells of a man made out of clay who was created by Rabbi Judah Loew, known as the Maharal, who lived in Prague in the 16th century. At that time there were often terrible attacks, known as pogroms, on the Jews of Prague. According to Jewish legend, the Maharal used magic to bring the Golem to life. The Golem guarded the Jewish quarter of Prague and protected the people from the danger of pogroms. There are many stories of the Golem's adventures. This one tells how the Golem was created, and how he was put to rest when he was no longer needed.

The other story by Peretz is "The Matchmaker." This story tells how the mysterious old woman, Sarah Bat Tuvim, sets up a match between the son of a nobleman and the daughter of a very poor charcoal-maker. Sarah Bat Tuvim is much like Elijah the Prophet, who often appears in Jewish folktales on some kind of mission to help a Jew in need. In making matches, Sarah Bat Tuvim is also fulfilling the will of Heaven, for it says in the Talmud that forty days before a person is born, a voice goes forth from Heaven to say that this one will marry that one, for such matches were believed to be made in Heaven. Readers will also recognize this tale as a version of "Cinderella," because the nobleman's son searches for a bride whose foot is slim enough to fit the slipper. This shows how Jewish stories drew on the folklore around them, but found ways to make it their own.

Among the Jews of Eastern Europe, there are many humorous tales about the fools known as the wise men of Chelm. Although Chelm was a real city in Eastern Europe, these stories are about an imaginary city where every inhabitant was a fool. There are two stories about Chelm to be found here, "The Wise Men of Chelm Move a Giant Hill" and "The Wise Men of Chelm Capture the Moon." These stories demonstrate that Jews have a fine sense of humor, and are even willing to make fun of themselves, since the fools of Chelm are all Jewish.

Then there are the stories about Hershele Ostropoler, who was just as famous in Jewish folklore as were all of the inhabitants of Chelm. Hershele is lazy and hates to work, so instead he plays tricks on people. These tricks are not exactly lies; but neither are they the truth. In "Half Price to Leitshev," Hershele pretends he is a coachman and tricks people into paying him to walk to the next town, instead of riding there. In "Don't Make Me Do What My Father Did," Hershele hints that something terrible may happen if the innkeeper and his wife don't give him a meal and a room for the night. In this way he plays the role of a schnorrer, a Jewish beggar who is full of tricks.

All in all, the ten stories in this collection reflect the very kind of stories that were likely to be told by a grandmother or grandfather, and that were so popular among the Jewish children of Eastern Europe. These are the stories that are especially beloved, and deserve to be as well known to every Jewish child as Cinderella or Snow White. For the hopes, fantasies, and longings of the Jewish people are reflected in these stories, making them one of our most precious legacies.

The Boy's Song

Adapted from "The Boy's Song". Classic Chassidic Tales edited by Meyer Levin

Rabbi Israel, the Ba'al Shem Tov – "Master of the Good Name"– as he was called, felt a great sadness during the High Holy Days. He sensed that the prayers of the people lacked the strength to fly to Heaven. It was as though a dark cloud prevented them from reaching God's holy presence.

Yankel, a herdsman, lived not far from Rabbi Israel's synagogue in Medibuz. Yankel had only one child, a soft-spoken, graceful boy named Chaim. But Chaim, for all his sweetness, had trouble with his studies. Even after years of school, he could not read. The Hebrew aleph-bet remained a mystery to him. And since he could not read the prayer book, he could not pray.

After a few years, Yankel stopped sending Chaim to school, which was called *chayder,* and instead, sent him out to the fields to take care of the cows. Chaim wandered through the tall grass and looked up at the blue sky. The beauty of the world touched his heart and stirred his soul. One day he took a thick reed and made himself a flute. All day long, he played his flute. The gentle melodies were like the singing of the birds and the sighing of the wind.

But Yankel was troubled because Chaim would soon reach the age of Bar Mitzvah.

"My son must learn something about the Jewish religion," he said to himself.

So, during the High Holy Days, called *Yom Tovim,* Yankel got into his wagon and drove his son to Medibuz, where he hoped to speak with Rabbi Israel about Chaim. All through the ride, Chaim played his flute. He played happy, lively tunes because he was so proud of the new cap and the new shoes that his father had bought him. The Yom Tov spirit of joy was upon him.

On *Yom Kippur* – the most serious

8

day of the year for all Jews – Yankel and Chaim went to the synagogue of Rabbi Israel. Chaim carried his flute in his pocket and sat very still. He watched the congregation as they read from their prayer books. His heart was glad as they  sang their songs of praise and pleading. His father's voice was deep and he turned the pages of his *siddur* with tender care.

"Father," Chaim said, "I too want to sing. I want to play my music for God." He took his flute out of his pocket and stroked it gently.

But his father took the flute from him.

"You cannot play it, Chaim," his father whispered. The rabbi will be angry. "It is forbidden to play an instrument on Yom Kippur." He put the flute in his own pocket.

Tears came to Chaim's eyes, but he said nothing. At last it came time for the final prayer of Yom Kippur, *Neilah*. The candles that lit the synagogue trembled as Rabbi Israel lifted his hands and spoke the words of the special Neilah prayer.

But even though the Rabbi's voice was strong, his eyes were sad. He realized that even his most devout prayers could not pierce the black cloud that seemed to hang over the prayer-filled room.

Chaim watched everyone praying and could no longer control himself. He seized the flute from his father's pocket and with great joy, began to play. The sweetest notes filled the synagogue as he played melodies that flowed from his soul – music that celebrated God's goodness and the beauty of the world He had created.

The worshipers turned to Chaim, angry and terrified. One man raised his fist at both Chaim and Yankel.

But the face of Rabbi Israel changed from sadness to joy. He motioned everyone to be still.

"Your music pierced the dark cloud and opened the gates of heaven," cried the Ba'al Shem Tov. "Because of you and your flute, our prayers have been heard and our pleas will be answered."

NOW CONSIDER THIS:

✻ *What do you think was wrong with the people's prayers?*

✻ *Why do you think the Ba'al Shem Tov allowed the boy to play his flute on Yom Kippur?*

✻ *Is there something special you pray for?*

The Big Sukkah

Adapted from "The Big Sukkah"
by Abraham Reisen

Baruch, a poor and pious Jew, lived with his wife, Tzivyah, and their many children in a small, one-room cottage. The roof leaked, and the mezuzah hung on a splintered doorpost. An unpainted wooden cabinet divided the room, and a huge oven took up too much space.

With the beds, tables and benches, there was hardly enough room to move. Tzivyah complained that it was difficult to keep an orderly house and prepare meals. Baruch often hit his head on the hanging cribs in which the smaller children slept.

There was no quiet corner in that crowded, noisy house where a man could study, a woman could dream, or a child could play. And sadly, when the circumcision of a newborn son was celebrated, there wasn't even enough space for the guests!

On holidays, Baruch and his family visited their wealthy relatives. They ate good meals in large rooms and talked quietly as the children played in different parts of the house.

Baruch was ashamed that he could not return his relatives' invitations. He knew that it was an important commandment to to welcome guests into one's home. Hadn't Abraham, our forefather, welcomed the angels?

But he also knew that there was no room in his tiny house for a large *seder* table on Passover, or a big Chanukah party with *latkes,* or a Shavuot meal with *blintzes.*

What was he to do?

One warm summer evening, an idea came to him. Sukkot!

While it was true that his house was very small, the yard next to it was very large. On Sukkot, he could invite his whole family, his rich cousins and his landowner uncle. He would build a sukkah as big as a palace!

Right after Yom Kippur, he and his sons attached two long rows of boards to

the wall of his house. The boards reached all the way across to his fence. Two brightly colored quilts became the door.

The family swept the ground and covered it with yellow sand. They carried all the furniture from the cottage into the big sukkah. The children decorated the roof of the sukkah with hanging fruit and hung garlands of fall flowers on the walls.

Tzivyah prepared delicious food in the cottage. It was easy to cook now in such a big, empty space.

Baruch invited all his relatives to have lunch with them on the second day of the holiday.

"What a wonderful sukkah," they all said. "Baruch, on Sukkot, this big sukkah is your palace, and you are the king."

Baruch smiled. "Yes," he said happily.

"My sukkah is the largest sukkah in the family. I am very happy to welcome all of you into it."

The landowner uncle sighed. "You are very lucky, Baruch," he said. "My own sukkah is so small, there's hardly enough room to move."

Baruch remembered those words all year.

From then on, he and his family happily shared holiday meals with his relatives in their large homes. He knew that on Sukkot he would repay their hospitality in his own big and beautiful sukkah. He too could fulfill the commandment of welcoming guests.

NOW CONSIDER THIS:

✳ *Why did Baruch feel ashamed that he could not invite his relatives to his house?*

✳ *If you could have anyone you wanted to come to your house, whom would you invite?*

✳ *What are some of the interesting symbols Jews use on Sukkot?*

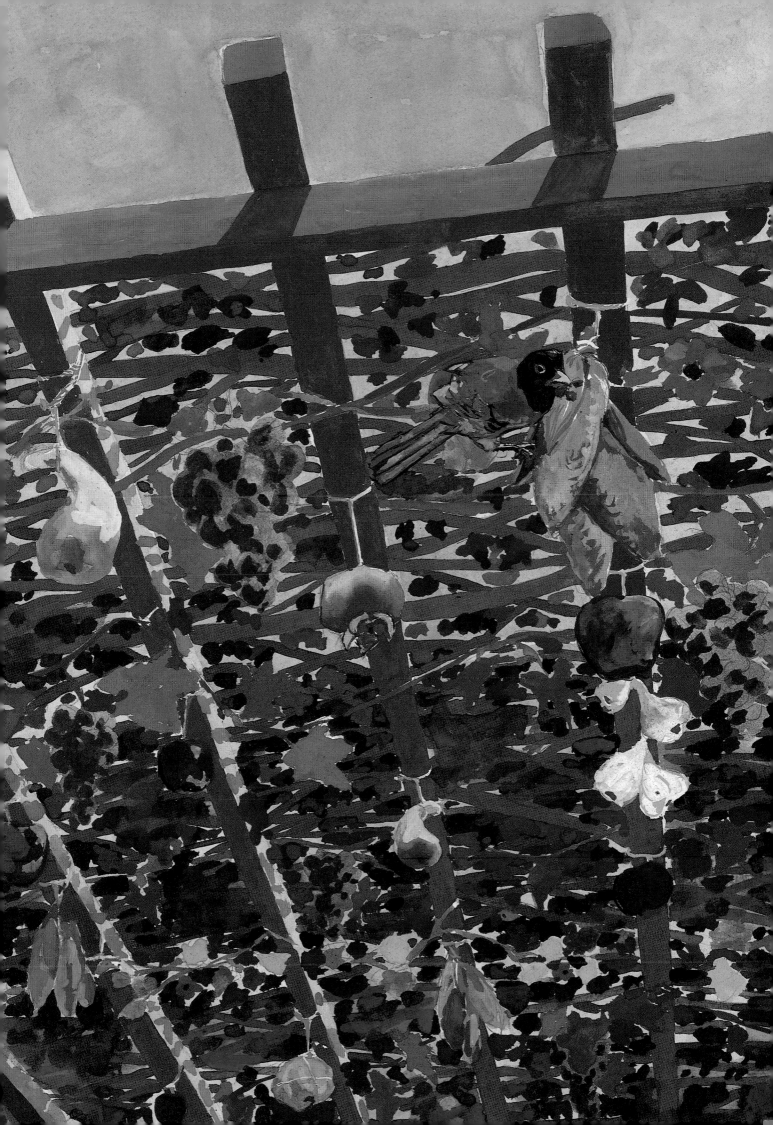

The Wise Men Of Chelm Move A Giant Hill

Some say that after God created the universe, He sent off an angel with two sacks filled with souls. One sack held the souls of the wise and the other the souls of the foolish. The angel distributed the souls evenly, so that there would be wise people and foolish people in every town and village. But as he flew over the town of Chelm, one of the sacks caught on the branch of a tree at the top of a hill and all the souls of the foolish spilled out.

And that is how the problems of Chelm began.

A giant hill, perhaps the same hill that the angel of God flew over on his way to hand out souls, rose up high in the middle of Chelm. It took up a lot of space. It blocked the sunlight during the day and, at night, it made it difficult to see the moon. The townspeople were annoyed by this, especially when the monthly blessing on the new moon had to be recited. If they couldn't see the moon they couldn't say the prayers, and that meant they wouldn't be able to fill an important commandment.

What were they to do?

They held many meetings to discuss this problem. At last, after a discussion that lasted for three days and three nights, one of the wisest men of Chelm got up and said:

"We have no choice! We must round up every able-bodied man, woman, and child and push the hill out of the village!"

"That's brilliant!" shouted another of the wise men of Chelm.

"I should have thought of that myself," lamented yet another.

"Tomorrow, we begin!" announced the wisest of the men of Chelm.

The next morning everyone gathered around the hill. It was a very hot day and as they pushed, they began to sweat. They took off their coats and cloaks and put them on the ground, out of the way. Then they went back to work.

They pushed and they pushed, cheering each other on when they grew tired.

No one noticed when a band of thieves crept into the town and stole their clothes.

"We've done enough for one day," one of the wise men said. "Let's finish tomorrow."

Everyone agreed, and went to get their clothes. But, though they searched and searched, they couldn't find their coats and cloaks.

"What has happened?" asked one of the wise men of Chelm.

"Don't you see?" said the wisest man in Chelm. "This is just wonderful!" he proclaimed, and clapped his hands with happiness.

"Tell us what has happened," everyone wanted to know.

The wisest man in Chelm got up on a chair, so everyone could hear, and announced, "We've pushed the hill so far back that we can't even see our coats and cloaks!"

NOW CONSIDER THIS:

✻ *If the people of Chelm are so foolish, why are they called "the wise men of Chelm?"*

✻ *What advice would you have given the wise men of Chelm in this story?*

✻ *The Jewish calendar is 354 days and is based on the moon. What things do you know about the moon?*

By Loving Man You Honor God

Adapted from "The Parables of the Preacher of Dubno"

A wise and wealthy man was the father of three sons. When his two elder sons were grown, they went to live in a distant town. The eldest son became very rich. He married and had many children and a large and splendid house. His younger brother, though he worked hard, was very poor. These two brothers seldom saw each other.

One day, the wealthy son received a letter from his father. The youngest son of the family was to be married, and, of course, the father wanted both older sons to be at the wedding. He wrote:

Please come home, my son, and bring your poor brother with you. I will pay for all the new clothing and repay you any money you spend on the journey. I do this because you will be obeying the fifth commandment of God, "Honor your father and your mother."

The wealthy son and his wife bought beautiful and expensive clothing for themselves and for their children. The boys and their father wore velvet suits. The girls and their mother wore brightly colored silk dresses. A carriage drawn by white horses was hired. But just as they were about to leave for the wedding, the children reminded their father that he had said nothing about the wedding to his poor brother.

Swiftly, the white horses galloped to the small house where the poor brother lived. Their arrival startled him. But the wealthy brother ushered him into the carriage even though he was still dressed in his shabby work clothes and tattered shoes.

When they arrived at their father's house, the townspeople came out to greet them. As the wealthy son and his family got out of the carriage, everyone admired their velvet suits and silk dresses. Silver buckles flashed on their shoes. Admiring strangers wondered who they were.

"Don't you know?" one of the

townspeople said. "He is the son of our town's richest man, and he is very rich, too."

At last, the poor brother slunk out of the carriage. He was ashamed because his clothes were almost rags and his toes poked their way through his thin shoes.

"And who is this one?" the strangers asked.

The townspeople turned away without answering.

As everyone entered the house, musicians played a merry tune in their honor. The mother and father hugged their sons. The wedding guests were very happy. They sang and danced to honor the bride and groom. But the poor brother did not dance. He watched sadly from a corner, hoping no one would notice his ragged clothing.

A week later, it was time to return home. The wealthy brother went to his father. He gave him a bill for the velvet suits and the silk dresses. He also gave him a bill for the carriage and the white horses.

"It is wonderful that you can afford such expensive clothes," said the father. "May your wife and children enjoy them in good health. And I hope you enjoy your ride home in that beautiful carriage."

"But aren't you going to pay these bills?" The wealthy son asked. "You promised to pay for all the clothing and for our journey. Here is your own letter saying so."

"Oh, I remember what I wrote," the father replied. "I promised to pay for everything because I thought you would fulfill the commandment to honor your father and mother. But your mother and I were not honored when you brought your brother to the wedding dressed in rags. Had you really wanted to honor us and bring us joy, you would have bought him a velvet suit like your own.

"All that you spent to come to the wedding was only for your own honor. Therefore I will not pay. I hope that this will teach you that you honor your parents when you show your love for your brother. You honor God when you show your love for man."

NOW CONSIDER THIS:

❋ *What ways can you think of to show people you like them?*

❋ *How do you honor your father and mother?*

❋ *If you had a poor brother or sister, how would you help them?*

❋ *What other commandments of God do you know?*

The Golem

Adapted from "The Golem" by I.L. Peretz

The beautiful city of Prague, the capital of Bohemia, sits on the shore of the Moldau River. The Jews of the city built a beautiful synagogue that they called the *Altneuschul,* the Old-New Synagogue. On the top spire of the synagogue were two clocks. The Jewish children of the city learned to tell time by studying the clocks, one of which had Hebrew numbers.

The Jewish community was very prosperous and many of the people even served as advisers to the king. Wise men studied in the city, and children learned in the many religious schools, called *yeshivot.*

The enemies of the Jews were jealous of the Jews and they spread evil stories about them. They even made plans to destroy the Jewish community. It became dangerous for the Jews to go out alone even during the day. Soon, the study halls of the yeshivot became empty because parents kept their children at home.

Everyone began to ask the same question:

"How can we protect ourselves from being attacked?"

But no one had an answer. Except one man, The Maharal, the great Rabbi of Prague.

One day he closed his books of learning, left the yeshiva where he studied every day, and went to the shores of the Moldau. He stopped at the best clay mound he could find, and carefully molded a giant human form with thick arms and legs and a lonely, watchful face. Gently he breathed into the figure's nose and whispered a magical, secret name into its ear. Then he called out to it, "Golem, arise!"

The Golem began to move. He rose up on his powerful legs, swung his great arms, and took long steps until he reached the streets of Prague.

From that day on, whenever Jews were in danger, the Golem appeared, ready to protect them and keep them safe. The evil people soon learned to fear the Golem, for he could snap the strongest clubs as if they were toothpicks and bend swords as if they were rubber. And, though they tried, the evil people could not hurt the Golem. Not at all.

Now that the people were safe, the Maharal returned to his studies. Fear faded from the hearts of the Jews. The children returned to the yeshivot, the merchants to the market, and once again things were calm and peaceful. The Golem continued to patrol the streets and to stand guard at the synagogue.

Weeks passed. The Jewish community was no longer in danger. But they had begun to fear the Golem.

"Please, Rabbi," the children of Prague pleaded. "Let the Golem rest."

One Friday, the great clock in the town square struck the noon hour. The Maharal sighed and closed his sacred books. He entered the synagogue and approached the Ark. In a high, yet strong voice, he began to sing: "A psalm, a song for the Sabbath day."

The Golem recognized the Maharal's voice. He came to the Maharal.

"You have done well, my friend," said the Maharal. "But now your work is done. Shabbat will be here soon. It is time for you to rest."

Once again the great Rabbi whispered into the ear of the clay giant. The eyes of the Golem closed, the breath left his body. All his power was gone.

There are those who say that until this very day, the Golem lies in a secret room in the Altneuschul.

He is hidden by spider webs so that no one can see him. He lies there, behind this gossamer curtain, waiting for the secret words of the Maharal to wake him.

NOW CONSIDER THIS:

✳ *Does the Golem remind you of any other creatures?*

✳ *If you had a Golem to command, what would you tell him to do?*

✳ *Why do you think the Maharal took away the Golem's power?*

Don't Make Me Do What My Father Did

Hershele Ostropoler stopped at an inn. He wanted to have dinner and spend the night. The innkeeper was away, and his wife was alone.

"I am very hungry," Hershele said. "Please give me something to eat."

The innkeeper's wife looked at his shabby clothes and his worn shoes. She did not think that Hershele would be able to pay her.

"I'm sorry," she said. "But I have no food."

"What?" Hershele's face was white with anger. "If there is no food, then I am afraid I'll have to do just what my father did."

The innkeeper's wife grew frightened. "What did your father do?" She asked.

"Never mind. You don't want to know what my father did," Hershele replied darkly.

The poor woman grew worried. Perhaps his father had been a robber, or even a murderer. Perhaps Hershele, despite his torn clothes, was actually the son of a noble- man or the king. She had heard stories of princes and kings pretending to be poor. If she did not give him food, he might call his father, and then.... Oh, indeed, she did not want him to do what his father had done.

Quickly, she set a table and gave Hershele a good dinner. When he finished, he smiled at her.

"I haven't had such a good meal since Passover," he said.

By then, the innkeeper had returned. He was a big, burly fellow with strong arms and a mean temper. He saw Hershele's shabby clothes and whispered to his wife, "I hope you took money from that beggar before you served him."

Just then, Hershele got up and said to the innkeeper, "I'd like my room now."

The innkeeper stared at him and said, "I'm afraid we have no rooms."

Hershele raised himself up and looked the innkeeper right in the eye. Then, waving his hands and shouting, he announced, "My dear fellow, unless you give me a room this instant, I will be forced to do what my father did!"

"What was that?" the innkeeper asked, beginning to feel afraid.

"Never mind. You don't want to know what my father did," Hershele answered in a menacing voice.

The innkeeper was now very worried. Hershele didn't look strong, but under those shabby clothes could be a trained fighter, ready to kill instantly. He didn't want to take any chances, especially with his wife around.

"Oh yes," he said, looking over his list of empty rooms. "I think we still have one room left." And he handed Hershele the key.

The next morning, as Hershele was getting ready to leave, the innkeeper and his wife got up the courage to ask him, "Perhaps you could tell us exactly what your father did?"

"Oh, my father?" Hershele replied. "Whenever my father didn't have any supper, he went to bed hungry, and whenever he didn't get a room, he slept in the barn."

NOW CONSIDER THIS:

* *Do you think it was right for the innkeeper and his wife to judge Hershele by his clothes?*

* *What trick did Hershele use to get the innkeeper and his wife to do what he wanted?*

* *Do you think the innkeeper and his wife laughed when they found out the truth?*
Do you think they were angry?
How would you feel if someone tricked you like this?

Half Price To Leitshev

Hershele Ostropoler was a lazy man. He hated to work. Unless, of course, he had to.

One day, his wife started yelling at him because she did not have enough money to buy even a chicken for their Shabbat meal.

"Do you want your children to go hungry?" she asked angrily. "Get up and go make a living," she scolded.

"All right, all right," Hershele said, getting up from his chair. "I certainly don't want my children to go hungry. I'll get you the money you need." Then he turned to his oldest son and said, "Go to our neighbor and borrow his whip. Meet me at the marketplace."

Hershele went to the town marketplace just as his son arrived carrying the whip. Hershele cracked the whip, and as people gathered around, he announced, "I'm taking passengers to Leitshev for half fare!"

People eagerly lined up for this bargain and gave Hershele their money.

"Here," he said to his son. "Give this money to your mother so she can prepare for Shabbat."

"Everyone follow me," he told the group who had paid for their trip to Leitshev.

"Where are the horses?" the passengers asked as they followed him down the road.

"Don't worry," Hershele said. "I'll take you right to Leitshev."

They followed him out of the city. Still, there were no horses. However, they were nearing the bridge, and they all thought the horses would be waiting there. But there were no horses at the bridge. By then they were almost halfway to Leitshev. It would be silly to turn back. Angrily, they followed Hershele.

At last they reached Leitshev.

"Give us back our money," the

people shouted at Hershele. "You fooled us."

"How did I fool you? I promised to take you to Leitshev, and here you are," he informed them.

"But we wanted to ride there, not walk," they complained.

"Then you misunderstood," Hershele replied. "Did I ever say a word about horses?"

The people grumbled, but realized that Hershele was right. He had never mentioned a word about *how* they would get to Leitshev, only that he would take them. And take them he did. Soon everyone went about their business.

Hershele returned home to a happy wife and a beautiful Shabbat table.

"Hershele, I don't understand," his wife said. "You had a whip, but where did you get the horses?"

"Ah," said Hershele, smiling. "You know the saying: 'If you crack a whip, you can always find some horses.'"

NOW CONSIDER THIS:

* *In what way did Hershele lie to the people, and in what way did he tell the truth?*

* *Do you think Hershele should have given the people their money back?*

* *What do you think Hershele meant by, "If you crack a whip, you can always find some horses?"*

* *Can you give an example of how people sometimes follow without thinking?*

The Matchmaker

Adapted from I.L. Peretz

a wealthy Jewish nobleman lived with his wife and son on a huge estate. He had everything he wanted, but still he was sad. He worried that his son would not be able to find a Jewish bride, for there were no other Jews living nearby.

One winter night a heavy snow began to fall. The nobleman was looking out his window and saw an old woman walking through the thick white snow drifts toward the house. She wore a high bonnet, and her thin shawl fluttered in the cruel, strong wind. She seemed to glide across the snow.

The nobleman and his wife welcomed her to their home. They prepared food for her and a comfortable bed. They gave her their best linens, their fluffiest pillows, and their warmest blankets.

"I only want to rest for a short while," the old woman said. "And I would like to pay you for your trouble."

"It is our pleasure," the nobleman's wife said warmly. "Thank God, we have all the money and riches we need."

The old woman smiled.

Later, as she was leaving the house, she turned to her hosts and said, "But surely there must be something I could give you?"

"Only God can give us what we need – a Jewish bride for our son. Each night, I recite special prayers to God, written by the wise Sarah bat Tuvim."

"Then God will surely help you," said their guest. "And I have a gift for your son's future bride."

She reached under her shawl and handed the nobleman's wife a pair of golden slippers.

"A gift from Sarah bat Tuvim," she said, and vanished into the night.

Many miles away, a poor Jewish charcoal-maker lived in a tiny hut in the heart of a huge forest. His wife was long dead, but his kind and gentle daughter kept house for him. When he could not sleep, she read to him the prayers of the wise Sarah bat Tuvim.

One night, after her father had fallen

asleep, the door to the hut suddenly opened, and an old woman entered. She wore a high bonnet and a thin shawl. Her eyes were bright, and she smiled tenderly at the girl.

"Don't be frightened," she said. "I am Sarah bat Tuvim, and I have brought you a gift."

She reached under her shawl and handed the girl a piece of velvet, satin threads of gold and silver, and pearls.

"Here," she said. "I want you to embroider a bag for your future bridegroom's prayer shawl."

Years passed and the nobleman sent his son out into the world to search for a bride whose slender feet would fit Sarah bat Tuvim's slippers.

He traveled very far for many years. At last he decided to return home, but he lost his way in a thick forest. It was Friday, and the sun was setting. He could not travel on Shabbat and was happy to see a little hut between the trees.

The charcoal-maker welcomed him and invited him to share his Shabbat meal. The young man noticed that his host saved a portion of his food and carried it outside.

"This food is for my sweet daughter," the old man explained. "She has no shoes, and she is ashamed to come in barefoot so she eats outside."

The young man took the golden slippers from his pocket.

"Perhaps these will fit your daughter," he said.

Minutes later, the charcoal-maker returned. "They fit," he announced happily.

The nobleman's son and the charcoal-maker's daughter were married beneath the stars. As they left the wedding canopy, an old woman wearing a high bonnet and a thin shawl came toward them. Her face was bright with holiness and happiness.

A match had been made!

NOW CONSIDER THIS:

✳ *Why do you think the Jewish nobleman worried about his son marrying a Jewish girl?*

✳ *What do you think makes a good match between two people?*

✳ *What other famous story does this story remind you of?*

The Magic Wishes

Three children lived in a small town in Poland. Yehudah was seven years old, his sister Miriam was six years old, and their good friend Shmuel was Yehuda's classmate.

Their teacher taught them that on the last night of Sukkot, Hoshanah Rabbah, the heavens open, and those who see it happen have one minute to make a wish. All such wishes are immediately granted.

"I would wish to be a great leader of my people, like Yehudah Ha'Maccabee," Yehudah said.

"I would wish to be as wise as the prophet Shmuel," Shmuel declared.

"And I," announced Miriam, "I would wish to be as wonderful and caring as Miriam, the sister of Moses."

They decided that they would stay awake all night on Hoshanah Rabbah, and when the heavens opened, they would make their wishes. On that holy night, they crept out of their beds and met in the synagogue courtyard. An owl hooted and small animals scurried through the underbrush. They were scared, but they waited. Hour after hour passed and they grew tired and hungry. At last, a clap of thunder rumbled, lightning streaked overhead, the earth trembled and the gates of Heaven opened.

In unison, all three children raised their heads toward Heaven. But by then they were so hungry and frightened, they forgot their wishes.

"I'm starved," Miriam said. "If only I had a knish."

Instantly a knish floated before them.

"How could you have wasted your wish like that?" Yehudah asked angrily. "You're such a foolish girl. I wish you were a knish!"

Pop! Instantly, poor Miriam turned into a knish, her lovely face trapped in the thick white dough. Her blue eyes filled with tears.

"Oh," cried Shmuel. "This is terrible. I wish Miriam were Miriam again."

Pop! The dough fell away and Miriam was as she had been. Another shaft of lightning rocketed through the sky and again a clap of thunder sounded. The children looked up. But the magic moment of wishes was over. Disappointed, they tearfully headed home.

"What's wrong?" a white-bearded old man, who seemed to come from nowhere, asked.

Sobbing, they told him how they had wasted their wishes.

"You did not waste your wishes," he assured them. "Your wishes are still your own. But you have learned an important lesson. You must earn by hard work what you thought would be granted to you by wishing alone."

"Who are you?" the children asked.

"I am called 'Shomer HaLailah' – the Guardian of the Night," the old man said, and he vanished.

The children found themselves back in their homes. They hurried to bed. But first, they promised each other that they would do as the old man had advised.

Yehudah studied very hard and became an adviser to kings and princes. He was known throughout the world for his wisdom.

Shmuel became a great scholar and grew famous for his knowledge of the Torah and the Talmud. He became a rabbi and married Miriam, who was both wonderful and caring.

During their wedding a white-bearded man appeared. He carried a lantern in one hand, a staff in the other, and he wore a wide sash.

The old man gave his lantern to Shmuel. "This will cast its light upon the Torah, so you may increase your wisdom" he said.

Yehudah received the staff. "This will protect you from your enemies," promised the old man.

Then he placed his sash in Miriam's hand. "Let this sash bind you to your people forever," he told her.

Through the years, Yehudah, Shmuel and Miriam used the items the old man gave them to help the Jewish people.

The three friends taught their children and their grandchildren to work hard so that their own wishes might come true.

Before he died, Rabbi Shmuel told his congregation what had happened to him when he was a small boy, on the night of Hoshanah Rabbah.

"Only you can make your wishes come true," he declared. "The key to the gates of Heaven is in your hand. Use it wisely, and you will discover all the riches that God has in store for you."

NOW CONSIDER THIS:

* *What wish would you have made if you were one of the children in the story?*

* *What do you think a Guardian of the Night does? How is he like an angel?*

The Wise Men Of Chelm Capture The Moon

Times were very hard for the town of Chelm. They had many expenses and very little money. Their old rabbi had died, and they wanted to provide for his family. The school needed a new door, and the ritual bath was leaking badly. How were they to get the money?

As was their custom, the wise men of Chelm met for three days and three nights and finally reached a decision. They would capture the moon and thus grow rich. After all, every Jew was required to say the blessing for the new moon. The people of Chelm would bring the moon down from the sky and keep it in their synagogue. Jews from all over would have to come to Chelm to pray because there is only one moon in the world.

"Imagine," said the wisest of the wise men of Chelm. "If we collect just one kopeck from each Jew in the world, each and every month, we will be richer than Rothschild!"

Everyone nodded in agreement, pleased with the wonderful idea.

But how was the moon to be trapped? It was suggested that all the ladders in the town be tied together end-to-end and placed on the roof of the synagogue. Then someone could climb up and grasp the moon. But what if that person were to fall? The people of Chelm would then have to support his family. They all shook their heads.

Perhaps a stranger could be asked to climb the ladder? No, the people of Chelm did not like that idea. They could not trust a stranger. He might steal their moon.

Finally, they decided to set a barrel of water near the synagogue on the night of a full moon. When its reflection hit the water, a thick sack would be thrown over the barrel, and the moon would be theirs.

And so, at midnight, as the silver moon glided through the starlit sky, the men of Chelm readied a big barrel of water. As soon as the moon rested on the surface of the water, they covered the barrel with a burlap bag and carried it inside. They danced around the barrel, happy in the knowledge that they would soon be rich. After all, the next time the blessing of the new month had to be recited, Jews from all over would flock to Chelm, their kopecks in their hand.

The people of Chelm could hardly wait. They were already planning to expand the city with the extra money they would receive.

Imagine their surprise when no one came on the night of the next new moon. A traveling merchant told them that the Jews in the neighboring towns had all said the blessings. The Chelmites were baffled. If they owned the moon, how was it possible for others to pronounce the benediction without coming to Chelm?

Finally, they uncovered the barrel. They were shocked and saddened to see that the moon no longer rested on the dark water.

"What kind of a world is this?" the wisest of the wise men of Chelm asked sadly. "The moon was ours, and we tried to keep it safe. Still, some thief stole it from us. There's no safe place to hide anything in this world."

NOW CONSIDER THIS:

✳ A blessing is a prayer of thanks to God because He did something good for us. What blessings do you know? What good things has God done for you?

✳ Why do you think the wise men of Chelm thought the moon and its reflection were the same? How would you show them the difference?

✳ Many Jews say special prayers every month when the new moon appears. Some say this is because the cycle of the moon – the way it appears and disappears in the sky – reminds us of the cycle of life. What do you think they mean by this?